ANDY GRIFFITHS

illustrated by Terry Denton

Feiwel and Friends • New York

A FEIWEL AND FRIENDS BOOK
An imprint of Macmillan Publishing Group, LLC

Our books may be purchased in bulk for promotional, educational, or business use. Please
contact your local bookseller or the Macmillan Corporate and Premium Sales Department
at (800) 221-7945 ext. 5442 or by e-mail at MacmillanSpecialMarkets@macmillan.com.

Library of Congress Cataloging-in-Publication Data

Names: Griffiths, Andy, 1961- author. | Denton, Terry, illustrator.
Title: The 65-story treehouse / Andy Griffiths ; illustrated by Terry Denton.
Other titles: 65-storey treehouse | Sixty-five story treehouse
Description: New York : Feiwel & Friends, 2017. | Originally published as The 65-Storey
    Treehouse in Australia by Pan Macmillan Australia Pty Ltd. | Summary: Andy and
    Terry travel through time trying to save their treehouse from highly talented, angry
    ants and Inspector Bubblewrap the building inspector while rushing to meet their
    publisher's deadline.
Identifiers: LCCN 2016027561 (print) | LCCN 2016055699 (ebook) | ISBN
    9781250102461 (hardback) | ISBN 9781250102478 (paperback) | ISBN 9781250102454
    (Ebook)
Subjects: | CYAC: Tree houses—Fiction. | Imagination—Fiction. | Authors—Fiction. |
    Illustrators—Fiction. | Humorous stories. | BISAC: JUVENILE FICTION / Humorous
    Stories. | JUVENILE FICTION / Imagination & Play.
Classification: LCC PZ7.G88366 Aam 2017 (print) | LCC PZ7.G88366 (ebook) |
    DDC [Fic]—dc23
LC record available at https://lccn.loc.gov/2016027561

Feiwel and Friends logo designed by Filomena Tuosto

Originally published in 2015 as The 65-Storey Treehouse
in Australia by Pan Macmillan Australia Pty Ltd

First published in the United States by Feiwel and Friends,
an imprint of Macmillan Publishing Group, LLC

First U.S. Edition—2017

10 9 8 7 6 5 4 3

mackids.com

CONTENTS

TIMELINE

The Present

The Present

The Present

The Present

650 Million BC

65 Million BC

65,000 BC

650 BC

65 BC

65,000 AD

650 Million AD

The Present

The Present

CHAPTER 1

THE 65-STORY TREEHOUSE

Hi, my name is Andy.

This is my friend Terry.

We live in a tree.

Well, when I say "tree," I mean treehouse. And when I say "treehouse," I don't just mean any old treehouse—I mean a 65-*story* treehouse! (It used to be a 52-story treehouse, but we've added another 13 stories.)

So what are you waiting for?
Come on up!

Hee-haw!

QUICK-SAND

We've added a pet-grooming salon (run by Jill),

a birthday room (where it's *always* your birthday, even when it's not),

an *un*-birthday room where the longer you stay, the younger you get (so don't stay too long or you'll end up like a little baby),

a cloning machine,

TREE-NN (Treehouse News Network): a 24-hour
TV news center, featuring regular updates on all the
latest treehouse news, current events, and gossip,

TREE-NN UPDATE   BREAKING NEWS: WE'VE GOT A NEWS FEED . . .

a lollipop shop run by a lollipop-serving robot called Mary Lollipoppins (she serves every type of lollipop in the world—past, present, *and* future),

TREE-NN UPDATE **LOLLIPOP LUNACY!**

a screeching balloon orchestra,

an owl house with three wise owls (we don't always know what they mean, but that's because they're *so* wise),

AARDVARK! CHEESE STICKS! POOP-POOP!

an invisible level,

an ant farm (with 65 chambers),

and a bow and arrow level.

As well as being our home, the treehouse is also where we make books together. I write the words and Terry draws the pictures.

TREE-NN UPDATE ANDY AND TERRY ACTUALLY WORKING: RARE PIC!

As you can see, we've been doing this for quite a while now.

Living in a treehouse may not be for everybody . . .

but it suits us just fine!

CHAPTER 2

ATTACK OF THE ANTS!

If you're like most of our readers, you're probably wondering whether we have a building permit for our treehouse. Well, of course we do. Terry organized it. "Didn't you, Terry? Terry?! Where are you?"

"Ah, there you are," I say. "I was telling the readers how you got a permit for the treehouse."

"GRRRR!" says Terry.

"Terry," I say, "quit messing around."

"GRRRRR!"

He looks kind of weird. And I think I know why. He's covered in ants!

TREE-NN UPDATE   ANT-COVERED TERRY ACTING KIND OF WEIRD

"Have you been playing in the ant farm again?"
I say.

But Terry doesn't answer. He just reaches out and grabs me by the throat.

"TERRY?!" I gasp.

Just when I can hardly breathe a moment longer, *another* Terry rushes in.

"Don't worry, Andy," says the second Terry. "I'll save you!"

TWO-TERRY TERROR!

The second Terry whacks the first Terry with a
badminton racket. WHAP!

And all of a sudden the air is filled with . . .

TREE-NN
UPDATE

ANTS!

There are ants everywhere (which is bad). But I'm not being strangled anymore (which is good).

"Are you okay, Andy?" says Terry.

"Yes," I say. "I think so, but what's going on? Why did you attack me like that?"

"That wasn't *me*," says Terry. "It was the ants *pretending* to be me. I accidentally left the ant-farm gate open and they escaped. I tried to get them all back in but they made themselves into a fake me and knocked me out. Then they must have come after you."

"But why?" I say. "I didn't do anything to them!"

"Me neither," says Terry. "All I know is that now they've turned into a giant foot and are about to stomp on us! Run!"

STOMP! STOMP!

"What are we going to do?" says Terry.

"There's only one thing we *can* do," I say. "Become dog poop, of course!"

"Dog poop?" says Terry. "But I *hate* dog poop!"

"So do *feet*," I say. "They will do anything to avoid stepping in it."

"Okay," says Terry. "How do we do it?"

"Simple," I say. "Just make yourself soft, squishy, and *really* stinky."

   DARING DOG-POOP DISGUISE!

"How's this?" says Terry. "Stinky enough for you?"

"Perfect," I say. "Perfectly *disgusting*."

And, sure enough, the ant foot stops stomping and just hovers cautiously in the air above us.

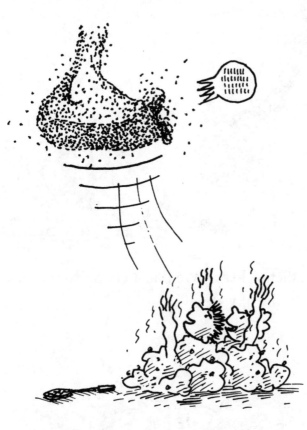

"It's working!" says Terry. "They can't squash us now!"

"No," I say, "not unless they change shape again."

"Oh no," says Terry. "They *are* changing shape again—into a giant pooper-scooper!"

"No problem," I say. "We'll just change ourselves into a puddle of water."

"We'll be safe now," I say. "Pooper-scoopers can scoop up poop . . . but they can't scoop up water!"

"We really fooled those ants," I say.

"Yeah," says Terry. "Ants may be smart, but we're even smarter."

"But maybe not quite smart enough," I say. "Now the ants are becoming a giant paper towel. They're going to absorb us!"

"But I *like* being water!" says Terry. "I don't want to be absorbed."

"Me neither," I say. "But we will be unless we change back into us . . . right now!"

TREE-NN
UPDATE

ABSORPTION DANGER: HIGH

We change back. We don't get absorbed (which is good). But we do get scrunched up (which is bad).

"If only we had some fire," says Terry, "we could burn the paper."

"I've got a match," I say, "but I don't have a matchbox."

"That's too bad," says Terry. "Because I've got a matchbox, but I don't have a match."

"Hmmm," I say.

"Hmmm," says Terry.

"Hmmm."

"Hmmm."

"Hmmm."

"Hmmm."

"Hey," I say, "I've got a great idea!"

"What?" says Terry.

"Why don't we put my match and your matchbox together?"

"That sounds dangerous," says Terry. "It might start a fire."

"Exactly!" I say. "Take *that*, ants!"

"It's working!" says Terry. "The paper towel is burning up!"

"Yes," I say. "But I think we're burning up, too!"

"Yeah," says Terry. "My head is getting *quite* hot."

"That's probably because your hair is on fire," I say.

"So is yours," says Terry.

"AAAGGGGHHHH!" we scream.

But we don't scream for long, because next thing we know the ants turn into a giant hose and start blasting us and themselves with cool, fresh, fire-quenching ant-water!

They blast and they blast and they keep on blasting until we are trapped at the top of a gushing geyser of angry ants.

"What do we do now?" says Terry.

"Call for help," I say, "and hope like crazy that Jill hears us."

CHAPTER 3

JILL TO THE RESCUE

"Help!" I yell.

"Help!" yells Terry.

"Andy?" says a familiar voice. "Terry? What are you doing up there?"

It's Jill!

"The ants went crazy and turned into a hose!" I say.

"Can you turn the tap off so we can get down?" says Terry.

"Sure thing," says Jill.

TREE-NN UPDATE   **JILL TO TURN OFF TAP!**

Jill turns the hose off (at the ant-tap) . . .

and Terry and I fall to the ground with a loud
THUMP!

"What did you do to upset the ants?" says Jill. "They appear to be very agitated."

"It's Terry's fault," I say. "He left the ant-farm gate open and all the ants got out and started attacking us."

"I only left it a *little* bit open," says Terry.

Jill frowns. "When it comes to ants," she says, "a little can be a lot. I'd better have a talk with them."

She gets down on her knees, makes her fingers into pretend antennas, and wiggles them around.

"It's not working," she says. "I'm too big. I need to be ant-size. Can you draw me smaller, Terry?"

"Sure, Jill," says Terry. "One ant-size you coming up!"

Soon Jill is deep in conversation with the ants—
which is not surprising, really, because Jill can talk
to *any* animal . . . even insects, and ants *are* insects,
which is why she can talk to them.

"What do you think they're talking about?" says
Terry.

"Beats me," I say. "I don't speak Ant."

Finally Jill turns to us and starts explaining, but her voice is just a tiny little squeak.

"Oh, great!" I say. "Now we can't understand her because she's too small."

"No problem," says Terry. "I'll give her this micro-mini-megaphone I made last week."

"Thanks, Terry," says Jill through the micro-mini-megaphone. "The ants said they are very cross because you and Andy keep wrecking their ant farm."

 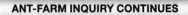 **ANT-FARM INQUIRY CONTINUES**

"But I'm always *really* careful around the ants!"
I say.

"Me too!" says Terry. "I'm even *more* careful than Andy!"

"And I'm even *more* careful than Terry!" I say.

"Well," says Jill, "that may be true, but perhaps you're not being as careful as you think you are. Take a look at this."

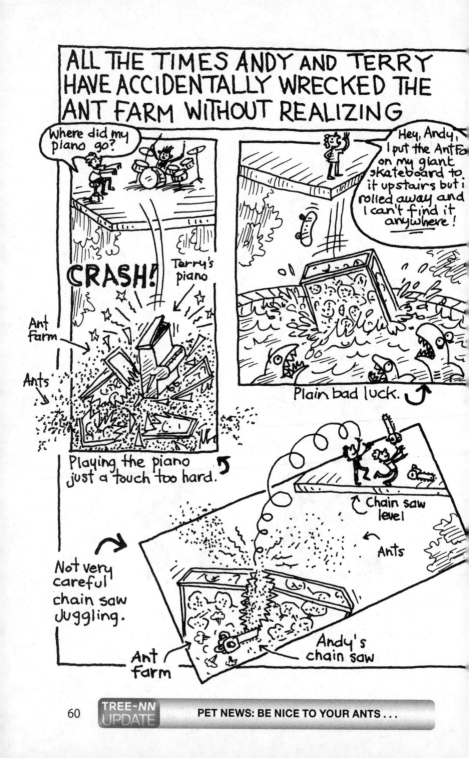

PET NEWS: BE NICE TO YOUR ANTS . . .

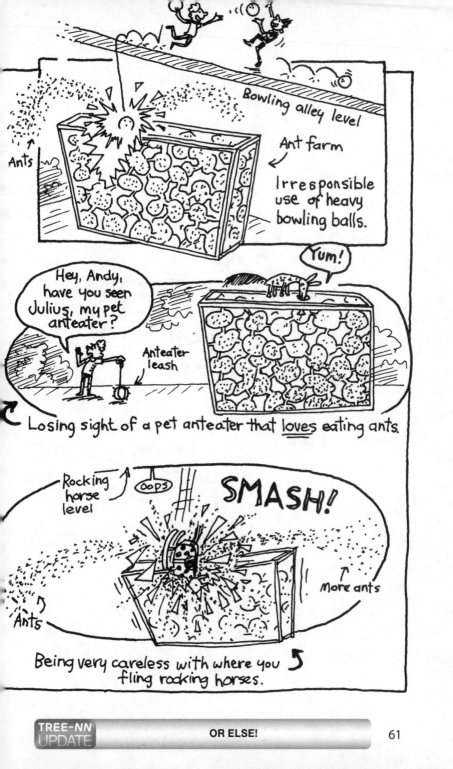

"Those poor little ants," says Jill. "You owe them a really big apology."

"I'm really sorry," I say.

"Me too," says Terry. "I'm really, *really* sorry."

"I'm even sorrier than Terry," I say.

"And I'm even sorrier than Andy," says Terry.

"I think the ants will be okay now," says Jill. "Just promise that, whatever you do, you WILL NEVER DISTURB THEIR ANT FARM EVER AGAIN!"

"We promise," I say. "Don't we, Terry?"

"Yes," says Terry. "We really, really promise."

"Good," says Jill, leading the ants away, back to the ant farm.

Now, where was I? Oh yes, that's right, I was telling you all about the permit. Like I was saying, Terry took care of that. "Didn't you, Terry?"

"What?" says Terry.

"The building permit. I was telling the readers that you organized it. You did, didn't you?"

"Well, er, sort of," says Terry. "Except for one small problem . . ."

"What problem?"
I say.

"I can explain,"
says Terry. "Once
upon a time . . ."

It should be
interesting
watching him
get out of
this one.

He-he.

(Hold on, readers, we're going into a flashback.)

SWIRL!!

"Once upon a time," says Terry, "you gave me some money to go and get a building permit for our treehouse.

"So off I went to the building permit office.

TREE-NN UPDATE   **UH-OH . . .**

"On my way through the forest, I met a friendly little man selling see-into-the-future peanuts . . . and, luckily, I had exactly the right amount of money to buy the whole bag!

"I didn't eat them, though, because I remembered that I'm allergic to see-into-the-future peanuts. So . . .

"I traded the see-into-the-future peanuts for the fastest horse in the world . . .

"but it wasn't fast enough so I traded it for a talking goat . . .

 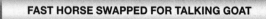

"but the goat only spoke French so I traded it for a singing monkey . . .

"but it turned out the monkey couldn't sing 'Happy Birthday' so I traded it for a solid-*gold* goldfish . . .

"but the solid-*gold* goldfish was so heavy it couldn't even swim, so I traded it for a mathematical mouse, but the mathematical mouse thought two plus two equaled five, so . . .

"I traded it for a performing flea . . .

"but the performing flea refused to do any tricks, so I traded it for a magic bean.

"After all that trading I was really hungry . . .

"*so* hungry that I completely forgot and I ate the magic bean."

HUNGER LINKED TO MEMORY LOSS

"You completely forgot what?" I say. "About getting the permit?"

"No," says Terry, "I completely forgot that as well as being allergic to see-into-the-future peanuts, I'm also allergic to magic beans!

"I didn't feel so good . . .

"and then I
felt worse . . .

"and then I
felt even worser . . .

WORD OF THE PAGE: *WORSER*

"and then, just when I thought I couldn't feel any more worser, I blew up!

"Now it's time to come back to the present."

"So you're telling me we don't have a valid building permit for the treehouse?" I say to Terry.

"That's right," he says. "But look on the bright side: I blew up but I didn't die."

"That's true," I say, putting my hands around his throat, "but you're going to die now. Any last words?"

"Yes," gasps Terry. "Who's going to answer the phone?"

"I will," I say. "And then I'll finish strangling you!"
I let go of Terry and answer the 3-D videophone.

(Did I mention we have a 3-D videophone? Well, we do—and it's 3-D!)

It's Mr. Big Nose, our publisher.

"What took you so long?" he says.

"Andy was trying to strangle me," says Terry.

"I'll strangle you both if your next book isn't here by twelve o'clock today," says Mr. Big Nose. "Good-bye!"

TREE-NN UPDATE **ANGRY PUBLISHER DANGER: EXTREME!**

"This is terrible," I say. "Not only do we not have a permit for the treehouse, but we haven't written our book and it's due today!"

"Look on the bright side," says Terry.

"What bright side?" I say.

"I *still* didn't die after I ate the magic bean and blew up," he says.

I go back to strangling him.

"Letter for you," calls Bill the postman, distracting me and accidentally saving Terry's life.

"Cool," says Terry. "I *love* getting letters."

We sit down and read the letter. This is what it says:

INSPECTOR BUBBLEWRAP
SAFETY CENTRAL HEADQUARTERS
BUILDING PERMIT DEPARTMENT

Dear Andy and Terry,

This is to inform you that I will be visiting your treehouse <u>in one minute</u> to check that you have a current and valid building permit.

Regards,
Inspector Bubblewrap

"What a nice letter," says Terry.

"Are you crazy?" I say. "He's a building inspector and he's coming to check if our treehouse building permit is current—the very building permit we don't have!"

"Yikes!" says Terry. "When is he coming?"

"In one minute," I say.

"One minute?!" says Terry. "Double yikes!"

CHAPTER 4

INSPECTOR BUBBLEWRAP

The doorbell rings and we go to answer it.

"Hello," says the man at the door. "My name is Inspector Bubblewrap. I trust you received my letter."

"Well, yes, we did," I say, "but—"

"Excellent," says the inspector. "May I please see your building permit for this treehouse?"

"Well . . . yes . . ." I say, "although when I say yes, I mean no. We don't actually have one . . . thanks to Terry."

"No permit?" says the inspector. "In that case I'll have to do an inspection to see if your treehouse conforms to all the current building regulations and safety codes."

TREE-NN
UPDATE

UH-OH . . .

"Building regulations?" I say.

"Safety codes?" says Terry.

"It's a mere formality," says the inspector. "Now, if you'll just be kind enough to let me in, I'll get started on my rhyme."

"Your rhyme?" I say.

"Yes," says the inspector.

"I always do
My reports in rhyme.
It's fun for me
And helps pass the time."

"Okay," says Terry.
"That's fine by me.
Please feel free
To see our tree."

"Well, thank you very much,
Young man.
I'll do my inspection
As fast as I can.

"If I may
I'll start right here.
Uh-oh—oh my—
Oh no—oh dear.

  TREE-NN UPDATE   **TERRY'S REPLY RHYMES, TOO!**

"*This staircase of yours*
Should have a railing.
And no wheelchair ramp?
That's a serious failing!

"*And where are your fire escapes,*
Your hose reels and sprinklers,
Your safety blankets and fire extinguishers?
And I'd very much like to see (if I can)
Your in-case-of-emergency exit plan.

"These man-eating sharks
Should be swimming free.
Not kept as pets
In a tank in a tree.

"And your bowling alley
Doesn't have any walls,
Which puts penguins at risk
From falling balls.

"Or a ball could fall
On a person's head
And that poor person
Could end up dead.

"Racing rocking horses
Around a track
Could result in injury
To the neck or back.

"This X-ray room
Is in direct violation
Of the current health
    and safety
Radiation regulations.

"And what sort of stupid,
    lame-brained twit
Would build himself
    a quicksand pit
And not even have
    the sense or wit
To put a warning sign on it?

"This swimming pool
Should have a fence.
(It really is just
Common sense!)

"And chain saw juggling
Is seriously dumb.
You could easily lose
A finger or thumb . . .

"Or an ear or a knee
Or an elbow or nose
Or an arm or a leg
Or a foot or some toes!

"Your trampoline
Has no net, I see,
And it's up really high
Near the top of the tree!"

"But, apart from those
few things," I say,
"is everything else
in our treehouse okay?"

Inspector Bubblewrap sighs and shakes his head.

"All things considered,
I'm sorry to say
There's no way I can issue
A permit today.

"This treehouse of yours
Is an unsafe construction
And I must insist
On its total destruction.

"A crew of wreckers
Is now on its way,
So you'd better get going;
There's no way you can stay.

"By twelve noon today
This place will be rubble.
If you stay any longer
You'll be in big trouble.

"It will all be knocked down—
Level by level—
Get out while you can.
You remain at your peril!"

"Yikes," says Bill the postman. "I'm out of here."

"Should we go, too?" says Terry.

"No way!" I say. "This is our home!"

"But it's going to be demolished!"

"Not if I can help it," I say.

"But how?" says Terry.

"I don't know," I say.

"Why don't we go and ask the three wise owls?" says Terry.

"Of course," I say. "They're so wise they'll know *exactly* what to do."

We jet-chair up to the owl house on our jet-propelled office chairs and hover in front of the owls.

"O wise owls," says Terry, "what should we do to avoid the total demolition of our treehouse?"

"TICK!" says the first wise owl.

"TOCK!" says the second wise owl.

"HOO!" says the third wise owl.

"Tick? Tock? Hoo?" I say. "What does that mean?"

"Hmmm," says Terry, frowning and repeating their words. "Tick-Tock-Hoo . . . Tick-Tock-Hoo . . ."

TREE-NN UPDATE   **TICK? TOCK? HOO?**

"Do you think Tick-Tock means something to do with time?" I say.

"Yes!" says Terry. "And Hoo must mean Doctor Who. He's a time traveler, right?"

"Yeah," I say, "but how does *that* help us?"

"Don't you see?" says Terry. "The wise owls are telling us we should travel back in time and get a permit for the treehouse."

"That would be a great idea," I say, "*if* we had a time machine."

"We do!" says Terry. "I've built one on the level the Once-upon-a-time machine used to be on."

"Fantastic!" I say. "Let's go."

We climb up to the time-machine level.

"So we go in here?" I say, heading for the door.

"That's not the time machine," says Terry. "That's an egg timer I built. I hate it when my eggs get overboiled. The time machine is over here."

TREE-NN UPDATE   **TERRY'S NEW TIME MACHINE: EXCLUSIVE PIC!**

"You put it in the trash bin?" I say.

"No," says Terry. "It *is* the trash bin."

"But why?" I say.

"Well, I was reading *The Time Machine* by H. G. Wells," says Terry, "and I thought that time travel sounded like fun."

"Yes, but why a wheelie bin?" I say.

"Because it's all I had," says Terry. "It's not quite finished but it should be fine to just go back a few years to get our building permit."

"You go first, Andy," says Terry.

I climb in and Terry climbs in after me and closes the lid.

"It's really cramped in here," I say. "I thought time machines were supposed to be small on the outside and big on the inside."

This is the outer wall of the bin. (Really!)

"Well, yeah," says Terry, "they are, but it was only designed for one person."

"You were going to go time traveling without me?" I say.

"No," says Terry. "Well . . . when I say no . . . I mean yes . . . but *no* . . . well, only a *little* bit . . ."

"How do you drive this thing, anyway?" I say.

"Easy," says Terry. "Set the chronometer for how many years back—or forward—you'd like to travel and then push the blastoff button."

"All right," I say.

I set the dial for six and a half years back. (That's just before we started building our treehouse.)

But at that moment the lid opens.

It's Inspector Bubblewrap!

"It's no use hiding, you know," he says.

"The wrecking crew are on their way.
They'll be here at exactly noon.
Get out and pack your belongings . . .
Or prepare to meet your doom."

"No way," I say. "We're staying right here."

"Oh, no you're not!" says the inspector.

He leans in and tries to grab us.

We crouch down as low as we can.

The inspector leans in farther, slips, and falls in on top of us.

TREE-NN UPDATE   **INSPECTOR BUBBLEWRAP TRASHED!**

"OUCH!"

"UGH!"

"OOF!"

There's a weird whooshing sound.

"What's that noise?" I say.

"I think the time machine has started," says Terry. "The inspector must have bumped the blastoff button as he fell in."

"Time machine?" says the inspector.

"Yes," says Terry. "Hold on, we're going back in tiiiiiiiiiiiiiiiiiiiiiiiiiiiiiiiiiiiiiiiiiiiiiiiiiiiiiiiiiiiiiiiiiiiiiiiiii iiiiiiiiiiiiiiiiiiiiiiiiiiiiiiiiiiiiiiiiiiiiiiiiiiiiiiiiiiiiiiiiiiiiiiiiiiiiii iiiiiiiiiiiiiiiiiiiiiiiiiiiiiiiiiiiiiiiiiiiiiiiiiiiiiiiiiiiiiiiiiiiiiiiiiiiiii iiiiiiiiiiiiiiiiiiiiiiiiiiiiiiiiiiime . . ."

SWIRL!!

CHAPTER 5

PREHISTORIC POND SCUM

We swirl for a long, long time.

Just when I think I can't stand it any longer, the swirling stops.

"We're coming in for a landing," says Terry.

WHAM!

The trash bin lands and we all fall out onto the ground.

"Have we gone back six and a half years?" I say.

Terry looks into the bin and checks the chronometer. "Oh no," he says. "We've traveled *650 million years* back in time!"

"But I only set it for *six and a half years* back," I say.

"The inspector must have knocked it when he fell in," says Terry.

"It's not *my* fault!" says the inspector. "That chronometer should have a safety guard on it. And a time-machine blastoff button without an emergency override directly contravenes Regulation 3, Subsection 4.5, Paragraph 6, Line 22 of the Time Travel Blastoff Button Act."

"I didn't even know there was a *Blastoff Button Act*," says Terry.

"Oh yes," says the inspector. "It's right here in this book, *Rules and Regulations of the World: Past, Present, and Future.* I never go anywhere without it."

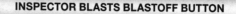

"Hey, Andy," says Terry, "look at this puddle. It's full of pond scum, and one of the pond scum looks just like you."

"You're right," I say. "And that one looks just like you!"

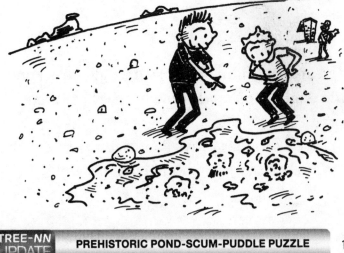

"Who are you calling pond scum, pal?" says Pond
Scum Andy. "You're not exactly an oil painting
yourself."

"Leave him alone," says Pond Scum Terry.

"Wow," says Terry. "Talking pond scum!"

"That's no ordinary pond scum," says the inspector. "These are the world's earliest simple life-forms. We're witnessing the beginnings of life on earth!"

"You got that right, pal," says Pond Scum Andy. "But it could be the end for us anytime soon."

"How come?" says Terry.

"Because the only thing keeping our puddle from drying up is that overhanging rock ledge."

I look up at the rock ledge Terry is standing on.
I see what Pond Scum Andy means; it *is* the only
shade around here, and the sun is *really hot*!

"That's too bad," I say.

"It's even worse for you," says Pond Scum Andy, "because if we don't make it, you'll never exist at all. At least we've had a life, even if we have spent it just floating around in a puddle. I mean, it's better than nothing."

"What do you mean we won't exist?" says Terry.

"If life-forms like us get burned up," says Pond Scum Terry, "then complicated life-forms like you will never get the chance to evolve."

"Oh no!" says Terry, looking really worried.

"Relax," I say, "they'll probably make it. They've got shade."

"But not for long," says Terry. "This rock ledge is cracking. I think it's about to break!"

"You idiot, Terry!" scream the pond scum as a large piece of rock breaks off and crashes down into the puddle.

"That puddle should have a sun shelter over it," says Inspector Bubblewrap. "It contravenes Regulation 456, Section B, Part 2 of the Prehistoric Sun Shelter Act. I therefore declare this puddle illegal!"

"What if we *built* a sun shelter?" I say.

"You'd need a permit for that," says the inspector.

"Can you give us one?" says Terry.

"Well, under the circumstances and given that the future of life on earth depends on it," says the inspector, "I think I could rush the paperwork through."

"Great!" I say. "Let's get started."

Pretty soon we've built the most amazing 65-story prehistoric pond-scum-puddle sun shelter you've ever seen.

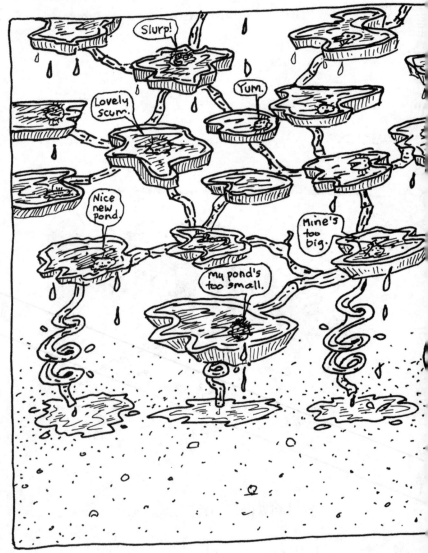

TREE-NN UPDATE   FIRST SUN SHELTER ON EARTH: EXCLUSIVE PIC

"There you go," says Terry. "That should keep you all sun safe for the next 300 million years or so!"

"Thanks, Terry," says Pond Scum Terry. "You're the best."

"No, Andy is the best," says Pond Scum Andy.

"That's where you're wrong," says Pond Scum Terry. "Because Terry is the best!"

"You're the one who's wrong," says Pond Scum Andy. "Because you don't know what you're talking about. Andy is the best. No contest!"

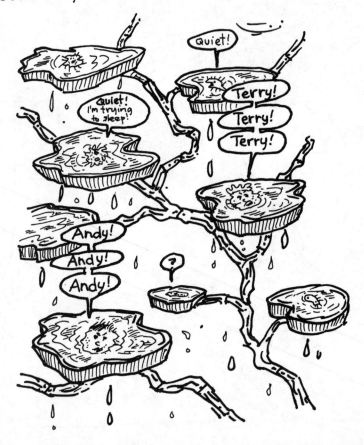

TREE-NN UPDATE **FIRST ARGUMENT ON EARTH: EXCLUSIVE PIC**

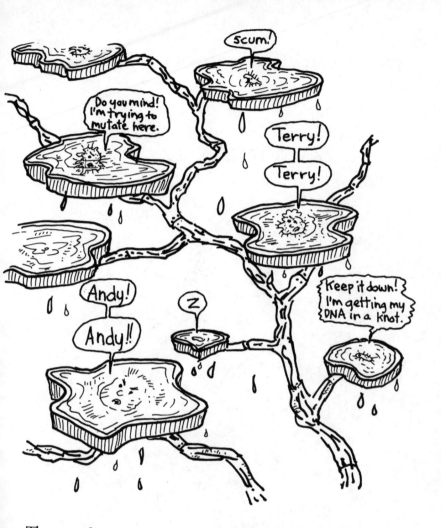

The pond scum continue shouting at each other.

"TERRY!"

"ANDY!"

"TERRY!"

"ANDY!"

Then things really get out of control.

"Let's leave them to it," I say. "We'd better be getting back to the future before this wheelie bin melts in the heat. It's pretty soft already."

"I hope our prehistoric pond-scum ancestors make it," says Terry.

"So do I," I say. "But if they don't and we end up not existing it'll be all your fault."

"But we *do* exist," says the inspector. "So they must have made it."

"Yeah," I say. "Thanks to me and my great idea about building a pond-scum sun shelter."

"And thanks to *me* for helping build it," says Terry.

"And thanks to *me* for issuing the permit," says the inspector.

"Speaking of permits," I say, "we'd better be getting to that permit office to apply for our building permit so the treehouse doesn't have to be demolished."

"Sure thing, Andy," says Terry. "I've set the chronometer for six and a half years before we left. Hold on, everybodyyyyyyyyyyyyyyyyyyyyyyyyyyyyyyyyyyyyyyyyyyyyyyyyyyyyyyyyyyyyyyyyyyyyyyyyyyyyyyyyyyyyyyyyyyyyyyyyyyyyyyyyyyyyyyyyyyyyyyyyyyyyyyyyyyyyyyyyyyyyyyyy . . ."

SWIRL!!

CHAPTER 6

DANCING WITH DINOSAURS

There's a loud splash and we look out to find ourselves floating in the middle of a vast gray ocean.

"Well, that's just *great*," I say. "Right time, wrong place."

"Actually, I think you'll find it's the wrong *time* as well," says Terry. "We've traveled to 65 million years ago."

"Oh dear," says the inspector. "Sixty-five million years ago? That's when a giant asteroid smashed

TREE-NN UPDATE   **ASTEROID DANGER: VERY HIGH**

into earth and killed off the dinosaurs. We are in one of the unsafest times *ever* in the earth's history!"

"Maybe the asteroid has already hit," says Terry. "I can't see any dinosaurs, can you?"

"Nah," I say. "But I'd really like to! Let's paddle to shore and see if we can find any there."

We paddle as fast as we can, but when we get to shore all we can see is a bunch of little monkey-like animals playing in a group.

"Ah," says the inspector. "They look like *Plesiadapis tricuspidens.*"

"Are they dinosaurs?" says Terry.

"No," says the inspector, "they're some of the earliest mammals to live on earth."

"They're *so* cute!" says Terry. "We should take one back for Jill."

"That's not a good idea," says the inspector. "They need to stay here so they can evolve into the ancestor of apes, monkeys, and humans."

"Monkeys?" says Terry. "I *hate* monkeys."

"Me too," I say, "but that doesn't mean we don't share a common ancestor with them."

"Ugh! Speak for yourself," says Terry. "I don't."

"I wouldn't be so sure about that, Terry," I say, "because that one looks a little bit like you."

"You're right," says Terry. "And that one looks a lot like you!"

  **MONKEY-LIKE LOOK-ALIKES SPOTTED**

Suddenly we hear thunderous stomping and snorting noises. The Plesiadapis stop playing and look around in alarm.

A dinosaur with an enormous nose bursts through the undergrowth and snorts at them.

"Yikes!" I say. "That dinosaur has the biggest nose I've ever seen!"

"It's a Bignoseasaur!" says the inspector. "A dinosaur that is in direct contravention of the World Health Organization's suggested guidelines for a healthy nose-to-body ratio. It's famous for its bad temper. The safest way to behave around one is to be very quiet and try not to be noticed."

"It reminds me of someone," says Terry, "but I can't think who."

"This is bad," says the inspector. "If the dinosaurs are still around that means the asteroid that wiped them out hasn't hit yet."

"Cool," I say. "We might get to see an asteroid!"

"If you do, it will probably be the last thing you ever see," says the inspector. "Asteroids are *very* dangerous, you know. Even more dangerous than Bignoseasaurs!"

"Hey!" yells Terry, as the Bignoseasaur advances on the Plesiadapis. "Get away from them, you big bully!"

At the sound of Terry's voice, the Bignoseasaur turns toward us. It stares and roars.

"Good one, Terry," I say, backing away.

"Yeah, good one, Terry," says the inspector.

The Bignoseasaur roars again and paws the ground.

"It looks just like Kevin the mechanical bull when he gets mad," says Terry. "I think it's getting ready to charge."

"If only we had a brightly colored cape," I say. "Maybe we could distract it."

"A brightly colored safety vest might work," says Terry.

"Don't be stupid," I say. "Where are we going to get a brightly colored safety vest from?"

"From the inspector," says Terry.

"Well, I'm not sure about that," says the inspector. "Regulation 6 of the Brightly Colored Safety Vest Act states that a building permit inspector should wear a brightly colored safety vest at all times."

"But it's 65 million years before that law was even invented," I say, "so, technically, you won't be breaking it."

"Hmmm," says the inspector. "Technically, you might be right . . . and I guess you will be using it in the interests of safety . . ." He hands me the vest.

I hold the vest out to the side, matador-style, and wave it at the Bignoseasaur.

It snorts in rage, lowers its massive nose, and charges at me.

I spin at the last moment and it rushes past.

"*Olé!*" I say.

SPORT: BIGNOSEASAUR "BULLFIGHT" BEGINS

It turns and charges again.

Once more I step aside.
"Olé! Olé!" I say.

Each time it runs at me and misses, it gets madder, and its nose gets bigger and redder.

"Watch out," says Terry. "I think it's going to blow!"
"What's that?" I say. "It's going to blow its nose?"
"No," says Terry. "Its nose is going to explode!"

TREE-NN UPDATE   BIG-NOSE-EXPLOSION DANGER: VERY HIGH

"Why, an explosion that big could wipe out all life on earth!" says the inspector. "Could it be possible that *this* is how the dinosaurs disappeared?"

"Who cares?" I say. "It's going to be how *we* disappear if we don't take cover!"

The Plesiadapis that looks like Terry starts biting the leg of his pants.

"Hey!" says Terry. "Quit that!"

Then the one who looks like me starts tugging at *my* pants.

"What's wrong with you stupid things?" I say. "Can't you see we've got a serious problem here?"

"I think they're trying to help us," says the inspector, who has one tugging at his pants as well. "They're pulling us in the direction of that burrow!"

"He's right!" says Terry. "And we don't have a moment to lose. I've never seen a nose so ready to blow!"

We quickly follow the Plesiadapis to their burrow.

Terry stops and bends over.

"What are you doing?" I say.

"I'm just saving a poor little helpless ant," he says.

"Well, hurry up!" I say.

Terry scoops up the ant and puts it in his pocket.

The entrance to the burrow is small, but with a bit of pushing and shoving we all manage to get safely inside.

"Cool burrow," says Terry.

"And *very* safe," says the inspector. "You can't beat a good underground bunker. And I see we have food supplies for some time."

"What sort of food?" says Terry.

"Looks like dragonflies, fern fronds, and a primitive form of marshmallow."

TREE-NN
UPDATE

AH...AH...AH...

"Prehistoric marshmallows!" says Terry, shoving a handful into his mouth and then immediately spitting them out. That's not marshmallow . . . that's fungus!"

"What do you think marshmallows are made of?" says the inspector.

But before Terry can register the full horror of what the inspector has just said, there is a huge explosion above us.

152

CHOOOOOOOOOOOOOOOOOOOOOOOOOOOOOOOO

We emerge from the burrow. There's an enormous smoking crater where the Bignoseasaur had been.

Everything is covered in thick green goo and there are piles of dead dinosaurs everywhere.

TREE-NN UPDATE   **LETHAL SNEEZE DEVASTATES DINOSAURS**

"Eurgh," I say. "Let's get out of here."

"But what about the Plesiadapis?" says Terry. "They saved our lives."

"And we saved theirs," I say. "Fair trade."

"But the prehistoric world is so dangerous," says Terry. "Can't we take them with us?"

"No, I already explained that," says the inspector. "If we took them with us, they wouldn't evolve and *we* wouldn't be able to exist. But just to be on the safe side—and if it makes you feel better—I'll give them all a bit of extra protection."

The inspector gets out his roll of bubble wrap and makes little bubble-wrap suits for all the Plesiadapis.

TREE-NN UPDATE   **FASHION: BUBBLE-WRAP SUITS ARE IN!**

"There," he says when he's finished. "That should keep them out of trouble for the next 65 million years or so."

"I've made a few adjustments to the chronometer," says Terry, "and I'm certain that this time we will arrive at the building permit office six and a half years before we left."

"I hope you're right," says the inspector, as we climb into the bin and close the lid.

"Me too," I say. "I think I've had enough history for one day."

"Okay," says Terry. "Here we gooooooooooooooo oooooooooooooooooooooooooooooooooooooooooooo oooooooooooooooooooooooooooooooooooooooooooo oooooooooooooooooooooooooooooooooooooooooooo ooooooooooooooooooooo . . ."

SWIRL!!

CHAPTER 7

STONE AGE ART SCHOOL

We swirl and swirl and swirl until, finally, the wheelie bin lands.

Terry is studying the chronometer.

"Well," I say, "is this six and a half years before we left?"

"Um . . . not exactly," says Terry, "but we're definitely getting closer . . . now we're in the year 65,000 BC."

I open the lid of the bin. "Wow, look!" I say. "*Cavemen!*"

"And *cave women!*" says Terry. "And *cave children* and . . . *cave dogs!*"

TREE-NN UPDATE   CAVE PEOPLE ROCK!

"They don't look very happy," I say.

"No," says Terry. "They look kind of bored."

"Well, it's no wonder, really," I say. "I mean, they are living in the Stone Age. All the really good stuff

TREE-NN UPDATE   LIFE BEFORE STUFF: EXCLUSIVE PIC

hasn't been invented yet. There are no books, no TV, no treehouses! There's nothing to do."

Terry goes up to them and says, "Hi, I'm Terry. How are you?"

"Bored," says a caveman.

"Why don't you draw something?" says Terry. "That's what I do when I'm bored."

"'Draw something'?" grunts one of the cavemen. "What is 'draw'? What is 'something'?"

"What is 'draw something'?" says one of the cave women.

Terry is shocked. "They don't even know what *drawing* is!" he says.

"It hasn't been invented yet, remember?" I say. "They don't have pens, pencils, spooncils, or paper. How could they know about drawing?"

"But what about drawing in the dirt with sticks?" says Terry. "They could do that. They've got lots of sticks and plenty of dirt."

Terry kneels down and starts showing the cave people how to draw in the dirt with a stick.

"Now you try," he says, giving them each a stick.

 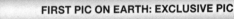 **FIRST PIC ON EARTH: EXCLUSIVE PIC**

The cave people try to do some drawings with their sticks, but (no offense, cave people) they're not very good. Even I can draw better than that, and I can't even draw.

"Here," says Terry, joining up the random marks one of the cave children has done. "I'll show you how to make that into a really cool picture."

The cave people get very excited.

"Do it again!" they grunt. "Do it again!"

So Terry does it again.

And they get even more excited.

So Terry does it for a third time.

"Now I'll show you painting," says Terry.

"'Painting'?" says a caveman. "What is 'painting'?"

Terry quickly makes a brush out of some stiff grass and a stick and mixes up some dirt and water.

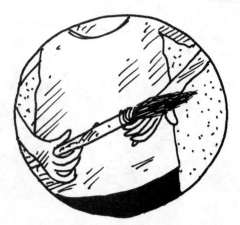

FIRST PAINTBRUSH INVENTED

"*This* is painting," he says. "You dip your brush in the mud and then daub it on the wall . . . like this."

A few of the cave people copy him.

"That's it!" says Terry proudly. "I think you've got it!"

It's not long before the cave people have covered every possible surface—ground, cave wall, and even skin—with drawings and paintings.

TREE-NN
UPDATE

CAVEMEN KANDINSKYS!

not a pipe

PREHISTORIC PICASSOS!

"Look!" says Terry. "They've done a Barky the Barking Cave Dog comic strip!"

"Oh no!" I say. "I hate Barky!"

"Don't be silly," says Terry. "Everybody loves Barky! Even cave people!"

"'Barky'?" says the inspector. "What's 'Barky'?"

"Only the world's most boring TV show!" I say.

"If you run along beside it really fast, it's just like watching a cartoon," says Terry.

"'Cartoon'?" says one of the cave women. "What is 'cartoon'?"

"See for yourself," says Terry. "Just follow me."

BARKY THE BARKING CAVE DOG
Me Sasquatc
Me trapped
stupid cave
Can't escap
Me leg bone.
Me got nothing
to say.
Bliss!
Me really
lost!

"Okay, that's enough now!" I say. "Let's go."

"Just one more turn?" says the inspector. "I love Barky!"

"See, what did I tell you, Andy?" says Terry. "*Everybody* loves Barky . . . even the inspector!"

"We have to go," I say firmly. "We've got a building permit office to get to."

"But I haven't taught the cave people about mixed media and installations . . . or performance art," says Terry.

"Don't rush them," I say. "There'll be plenty of time for that in the future. Come on!"

We climb into the bin and Terry starts adjusting the chronometer. "I think I've got it this time," he says.

"That's what you said last time," I say.

"I know," he says. "The six and the five are working fine. It's just the zeros I was having trouble with, but I'm pretty sure I've got them working nowwwwwwwwwwwwwwwwwwwwwwww wwwwwwwwwwwwwwwwwwwwwwwwwwww wwwwwwwwwwwwwwwwwwwwwwwwwwww wwwwwwwwwwwwwwwwwwwwwwwwwwww wwwwwwwwwwwwwwwwww . . ."

SWIRL!!

CHAPTER 8

MUMMY MADNESS

We swirl through time once more until we feel the now-familiar falling sensation.

Terry peeps out the top of the bin.

"Can you see the building permit office?" I say.

"Um," he says, "does the building permit office look like a pyramid?"

"No," says the inspector.

TREE-NN
UPDATE UH-OH . . .

"Then I think we might be in ancient Egypt," says Terry. "All I can see is sand, the Sphinx, palm trees, and a big gold-topped pyramid that we're about to smash into."

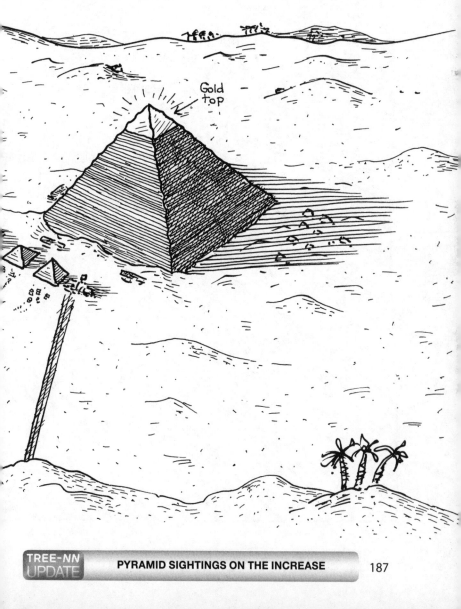

Gold top

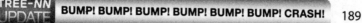

Finally, we come to a stop. A crowd of stunned-looking ancient Egyptians are staring at our bin.

"You idiots!" says one of them. "You just squashed the pharaoh!"

"Uh-oh," says Terry. "I think we just squashed the pharaoh, whatever that is."

"That's the king of ancient Egypt!" I say. "This is bad. Very bad."

TREE-NN UPDATE **PHARAOH FLATTENED BY FLYING BIN!**

The inspector shakes his head sadly. "If only people would take the trouble to install landing warning beepers on their time-traveling wheelie bins, this sort of unpleasant accident could easily be avoided."

The pharaoh lets out a loud moan.

"He's still alive!" says Terry.

"Quick, let's get the bin off him," I say.

We lift the bin off the pharaoh and help him to his feet.

"Thank you!" he says. "And now you must die!"

"But we just saved your life!" says Terry.

"You also just squashed me with your sky chariot," says the pharaoh, "and the penalty for squashing the pharaoh is death. Guards—seize them!"

  TREE-NN UPDATE   SKY CHARIOTEERS FACE DEATH PENALTY

"Now, just hold on a minute!" says the inspector.

"Who are you?" says the pharaoh.

"Inspector Bubblewrap's the name," says the inspector, "and inspecting buildings is my game." He hands the pharaoh his business card.

The pharaoh looks worried. "You're a *building inspector*?" he says.

"Yes!" says Inspector Bubblewrap. "Do you have a current and valid building permit for this pyramid?"

"Why . . . *er* . . . yes," says the pharaoh, "of course I do."

"May I see it?" says the inspector.

The pharaoh signals to a scribe, who brings over a scroll and hands it to Inspector Bubblewrap.

The inspector unrolls it and examines it closely.

"Is this *your* signature?" he says to the pharaoh.

"Yes," says the pharaoh. "I sign and issue all my building permits myself."

"This is highly irregular," says the inspector. "I've never heard of anybody signing their own building permits. I'm afraid I'm going to need you to fill out a few forms. It will take a few minutes of your valuable time. And I'll help you along with a form-filling rhyme."

"I'll need you to complete
This building certificate.
Use black ink or blue,
And I'd like it in triplicate.

"And don't forget to include
All your personal information:
Your star sign, your weight,
And your marital situation.

"I'll also require
All your contact details:
Your home phone, your address,
And both home and work e-mails.

"You'll need approval from council
So here's an application.
And if your neighbors object
You'll have to seek arbitration.

"I'll need to see blueprints
(From top to foundation)
And a 5,000-hieroglyph essay
In support of your application.

"You're an owner-builder,
So I'll need proof of your
    qualifications.
Even a pharaoh
Has to follow the regulations."

I nudge the inspector to get his attention.

"Is this really the best time to be worrying about whether the pharaoh has a permit for his pyramid?" I whisper. "Shouldn't we be trying to figure out how to avoid being put to death?"

"That's exactly what I *am* doing," says the inspector. "While he's busy with the paperwork we can make our escape. Come on, let's hide in the pyramid."

We run through the doorway behind us and down a long corridor into a dark chamber.

"I can't see anything!" says Terry.

"Me neither," I say. "And quit tapping me!"

"I'm not tapping you," says Terry. "It must be the inspector."

"It's not me," says the inspector. "I'm too busy looking for my flashlight."

"But if it isn't *Terry* and it isn't *you*, then *who* is it?"

"It could be a mummy," says Terry.

"Ah, there's my flashlight!" says the inspector.

He switches it on.

"I was right!" says Terry. "It *is* a mummy."

TREE-NN UPDATE AAAAAAAAAAAAGGGGGGGGGGGGGHHHHHHHHHHH!

The inspector turns off his flashlight. "Here," he says, thrusting a load of bubble wrap into my hands. "Wrap yourself up in this."

"Terry," he says, "you do the same."
    "But why?" says Terry.
    "No time to explain. Just do it."

We do it.
    The inspector turns his flashlight on again.

This time it's the mummy's turn to be scared. It turns and runs out of the chamber.

TREE-NN UPDATE   **FRIGHTENED MUMMY FREAKED OUT BY FAKES**

"Great work, Inspector!" I say. "But how did you know the mummy would be scared of other mummies?"

"Just a hunch," he says. "Let's go!"

We head for a door on the far side of the chamber, squeeze through it . . .

and fall straight through

a

trap-

d

o

o

o

o

o

o

o

r

!

We land in something soft.

It's too dark to see anything, but I can feel Terry wriggling around next to me.

"Mmmmm," he says, sighing happily. "Soft and squishy!"

TREE-NN UPDATE   WEATHER: SQUISHY WITH A CHANCE OF ASPS

"I'm not sure 'soft and squishy' is necessarily a good thing, Terry," I say. "Especially when it's hissing. I think we might be in a pit of asps."

"What are asps?" says Terry.
"Ancient Egyptian snakes!" I say.
"Yikes!" screams Terry.

"Let's not panic," says the inspector. "Fortunately, I still have my flashlight." He turns it on.

I was right.

We *are* in a pit of asps.

TREE-*NN* UPDATE AUTHOR PROVED RIGHT . . . YET AGAIN!

"Okay, that's quite enough screaming for one pit of asps!" says the inspector. "We're safely covered in bubble wrap so they can't bite us."

"Yes, but how do we get out of the pit?" I say.

The inspector shrugs and shakes his head sadly. "If only people would take the trouble to install emergency exits in their snake pits, this sort of dilemma could be easily avoided," he says.

"We don't need an emergency exit," says Terry. "We've got *asps*. We can charm them and use them as a ladder."

"Well, that's a great idea," I say, "but you need music to charm snakes, and as far as I know none of us brought our pungis."

"What's a pungi?" says Terry.

"It's a wind instrument used to charm snakes," I say.

"No, I don't have one of those," says Terry. "But I've got a balloon. That should work just as well."

Terry blows the balloon up, pinches the neck, and starts releasing the air in a high-pitched screech. Sure, it might not be everybody's idea of beautiful music, but the snakes seem to like it.

The snakes rise up, swaying and threading themselves together, until eventually they form a ladder that leads right to the top of the pit.

We scramble up the snake ladder as fast as we can and make it to the top just as Terry's balloon runs out of screech and the ladder collapses.

TREE-NN UPDATE SNAKE LADDER A SUPER SUCCESS

"Wow," says Terry, panting, "that was even more fun than our snakes and ladders level back in the treehouse!"

"I'm not sure that 'fun' is exactly the word I would use," says the inspector, "but, I must admit, I do feel quite . . . unusually . . . *energized!*"

I can hear shouting somewhere behind us.

"We'd better keep moving," I say. "I think the pharaoh might have finished his paperwork."

We run down a long corridor, keeping a careful watch for mummies and trapdoors.

"Look!" says Terry, pointing to a series of pictures on the wall. "It's Barky the Barking Dogyptian!"

 ANCIENT "BARKY" CARTOON TOMB DISCOVERY

At the end of the corridor we come across two ancient Egyptians working on the Barky cartoon.

"It's us again!" says Terry. "Hi, Ancient Egyptian Andy and Terry!"

"Who are you?" says Ancient Egyptian Andy.

"We're your future selves!" I explain.

"Pleased to meet you!" says Ancient Egyptian Andy.

"Great Barky the Barking Dogyptian cartoon!" says Terry.

"Thanks!" says Ancient Egyptian Terry.

Ancient Egyptian Andy rolls his eyes. "I think it's dumb," he says.

"I agree," I say. "High-five, Ancient Egyptian Andy!"

"Well, we'd love to stay and chat," I say, "but we're being chased by the pharaoh's guards. Is there a fast way out of here?"

"Sure," says Ancient Egyptian Terry. He quickly scribbles a map on a piece of papyrus and hands it to me. "Just follow this."

We say good-bye to our ancient Egyptian selves and follow the map until at last we are back outside in the ancient Egyptian sunlight. We peel off our bubble wrap as fast as we can. (That stuff is hot!)

"Thank goodness we're out of there," I say.

"Yes," says the inspector. "That pyramid is so dangerous it makes the treehouse look positively safe!"

"Uh-oh," I say. "Here come the guards. Run!"

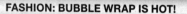

We run. Behind us we hear the popping of the bubble wrap as the guards step on it.

"Hey, this stuff is *fun!*" says one.

They all stop, pick up handfuls of bubble wrap, and start popping it like crazy.

We reach the bin and climb in, and Terry resets the chronometer. We blast off and zoom up into the air through a cloud of sand.

"Phew!" says the inspector. "That was a close one." He takes off his hard hat and wipes his brow. "Oh dear . . ."

TREE-NN UPDATE   **TIMELY ESCAPE FOR TIME-TRAVELING TRIO**

"What's the matter?" I say.

"There's an asp," he says.

"Where?"

"In my hat . . . no . . . hang on, it's not in my hat anymore. It's in the bin somewhere."

"YIKES!" screams Terry. The bin swerves out of control and heads toward a giant stone nose—the nose of the Great Sphinx!

"Terry, watch out!" I yell.

But it's too late.

"Oops," says Terry.

"So *that's* how the Sphinx lost its nose," says the inspector.

"Another mystery solved!" says Terry.

ALL THE MYSTERIES WE HAVE SOLVED

1. The Mystery of the Angry Ants ~~CASE CLOSED~~

2. The Mystery of the Missing Building Certificate ~~CASE CLOSED~~

3. The Mystery of How Dinosaurs Really Became Extinct ~~CASE CLOSED~~

4. The Mystery of the Shoulder Tapper ~~CASE CLOSED~~

5. The Mystery of How the Sphinx Lost Its Nose ~~CASE CLOSED~~

"That's all very well," I say, "but there's still an asp in the bin!"

"Not for long, though," says the inspector. He scoops the asp up in his hard hat and flings both the asp and his hat overboard.

"Wow, that was brave!" I say. "And risky!"

"And just in time," says Terry. "Hold on, here we go againnnnnnnnnnnnnnnnnnnnnnnnnnnnnnnnnn nnnnnnnnnnnnnnnnnnnnnnnnnnnnnnnnnnnnnnn nnnnnnnnnnnnnnnnnnnnnnnnnnnnnnnnnnnnnnn nnnnnnnnnnnnnnnnnnnnnnnnnnnnnnnnnnnnnnn nnnnnnnnnnnnnnnnnnnnn . . ."

SWIRL!!

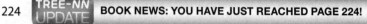

CHAPTER 9

BIN-HUR

We swirl through time until the chronometer reads 65 BC and we start plummeting toward the ground. We land but this time we don't stop moving. I peep out of the bin and realize why.

We're hurtling along a chariot racing track in the middle of an ancient Roman chariot race and, surprisingly, we don't seem to be doing that badly. It looks like we're in fourth place.

"Oh dear," says the inspector. "This looks dangerous."

"Hey, look," says Terry, "an Ancient Roman Andy and an Ancient Roman Terry!"

Terry's right! Ahead of us are two chariots—one being driven by someone who looks a lot like Terry and the other by someone who looks a lot like me.

Coming up behind them is a scary-looking woman driving a chariot with big spikes on its wheels.

She is getting closer and closer to Ancient Roman Andy's chariot, and then the metal spike crashes through his wheel and smashes it to pieces!

His chariot skids wildly and tips over. Ancient Roman Andy is thrown from his chariot onto the racetrack.

TREE-NN UPDATE **SPIKED WHEELS MAY BE HAZARDOUS TO HEALTH**

He's still holding on to his horse's reins, though, and is being dragged along on his stomach.

"Ouch," I say. "That's gotta hurt!"

Our bin is slowing down but we're still moving fast enough to catch up to him.

I lean out and reach toward him. "Give me your hand," I say.

"What the maximus?" he says. "Who are you?"

"No time to explain," I say. "Just do it."

He reaches up with one hand while still holding his reins in the other. The inspector and Terry hold on to me as I lean out and pull him into the bin.

TREE-NN UPDATE   **ANCIENT ROMAN RESCUE ATTEMPT!**

"I am Andronicus Grillius," he says, "and I thank you." He snaps the reins. "YAH!" he yells, urging his horse on.

With Andronicus driving, we are going much faster than we were before. We're back in the race!

"We must beat Drusilla the Dreadful," says Andronicus, pointing to the driver of the chariot with spiked wheels. "She is the most feared and ruthless charioteer in Rome—she has already destroyed almost all the others."

TREE-NN UPDATE   **DRUSILLA THE DREADFUL TIPPED TO WIN RACE**

He's not kidding. There is chariot wreckage everywhere.

"Those spiked wheels seem very dangerous," says the inspector. "Surely there must be rules of some sort! It just doesn't seem right."

"Alas," says Andronicus, "chariot-racing rules have not been invented yet, and now she is after my friend Terencius Densus."

Drusilla is gaining on the only other chariot (apart from ours) left in the race.

She drives in close and uses her wheel spike to destroy Terencius's wheel. He jumps from his wrecked chariot onto his horse and rides after Drusilla.

  DENSUS DOWN BUT NOT DEFEATED

Andronicus drives our bin up beside Terencius.
"Join us, friend," he calls.

Keeping hold of his horse's reins, Terencius leaps
into our bin.

"This is highly irregular," says the inspector. "The
maximum capacity for a bin this size is four. We'd
better not take on any more passengers."

"Don't worry," I say. "There's nobody else left to
take on. It's just us versus Drusilla now."

With two horses pulling us we're really starting to gain on Drusilla.

She looks back and glares at us.

"I don't like her," says Terry.

"Me neither," says Terencius. "Nobody does."

As we draw level, Drusilla the Dreadful veers toward us in order to wreck our bin with her terrible wheel spike. "*Tibi delenda*, losers!" she snarls.

"What does that mean?" says Terry.

"'You must be destroyed, losers,'" says Andronicus.

TREE-NN UPDATE   **NEW POLL SHOWS DRUSILLA 100% DISLIKED**

"Not on my watch," says the inspector, unfurling a long roll of bubble wrap. "Hold on to me, lads!" he says.

Terencius takes the reins while the rest of us hold on to Inspector Bubblewrap.

The inspector leans out, his head only centimeters from the lethal spinning spike . . .

and holds out the bubble wrap. The wheel spike on Drusilla's chariot catches the end of the bubble wrap. As it spins, it wraps the bubble wrap around itself, rendering the spike completely harmless.

Terencius maneuvers our bin around to the other side of Drusilla's chariot and the inspector bubble-wraps that spike as well.

We pull the inspector back into the bin.

"Way to go, Inspector!" says Terry.

"That is the most dangerous thing I've ever seen anybody do!" says Andronicus.

Inspector Bubblewrap smiles proudly and says:

*"I'm a safety inspector,
That's what I do:
I make things safe
For me and you.*

*"I'll risk my life,
If that's what it takes,
To make things safe
For all our sakes."*

Now the race gets *really* serious.

242 TREE-NN UPDATE   TWO LAPS TO GO!

"This is the final lap," says Andronicus. "We have done well, but Drusilla is going to win!"

"If only we could get past her," says Terencius.

Back end of horse.

"We can't go past her," says the inspector. "But we can go *over* her!"

"How?" I say.

"By using that pile of destroyed chariots as a ramp," he says. "That's how."

"Are you sure?" says Terry. "That sounds kind of dangerous."

"Of course I'm sure," says the inspector. "If there's one thing I know about, it's ramps: wheelchair-access ramps, freeway ramps, curb ramps, folding ramps, boat ramps. Trust me, I know ramps."

Inspector Bubblewrap takes the reins from Terencius and steers our wheelie bin toward an especially big pile of crashed chariots.

"Everybody hold on tight!" shouts the inspector.

We rocket up the "ramp" and fly through the air. We sail up and over Drusilla . . .

 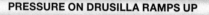 **PRESSURE ON DRUSILLA RAMPS UP**

and cross the finish line. First!

The crowd goes crazy.

The emperor rises to his feet and gives us two thumbs-up, which makes the crowd go even crazier.

TREE-NN UPDATE **TWO THUMBS-UP FOR TREEHOUSE DREAM TEAM**

"We won!" says Andronicus. "Thanks to you, we won't be put to death."

"You were going to be *killed*?!" says Terry.

"Yes," says Terencius. "But Caesar Proboscis Maximus has spared us. That's what the two thumbs-up means."

"Wow," says Terry, "ancient Rome is a *really* dangerous place."

"Yes," says the inspector, "but it's a little bit safer now, thanks to bubble wrap."

Andronicus and Terencius climb out of the bin.

"Thank you for your bravery, Inspector Bubblewrapus," says Andronicus.

"We owe you our lives," says Terencius, "for you saved us with your courage, your knowledge of ramps, and your strange, clear material with its many air pockets."

"That was an exciting race," says Terry. "It would make a great scene in a movie about ancient Rome."

"It already has," I say.

"Cool," says Terry. "Can we watch it when we get back to the treehouse?"

"Sure," I say. "*If* we ever get back to the treehouse. But before we can do that we have to get to the building permit office."

"We'll get there this time for sure," says Terry, "or my name's not Terencius Densus."

"But it's *not* Terencius Densus," I remind him.

"Uh-oh," he says, as everything starts to swirllllll
llllllllllllllllllllllllllllllllllllllllllllllllllllllllllllllllllllllllllllllll
llllllllllllllllllllllllllllllllllllllllllllllllllllllllllllllllllllllllllllllll
llllllllllllllllllllllllllllllllllllllllllllllllllllllllllllllllllllllllllllllll
lllllllllllllllllllllllllllllllllllllllllllll . . .

SWIRL!!

CHAPTER 10

THE FUTURE

The swirling stops and we slowly fall to the ground.

"Wow, smooth landing, Terry," I say.

"Yeah," he says. "It's like we practically *floated* down."

I look at the gravity detector gauge on the instrument panel. "That's because we *did* float down," I say. "Gravity is only one-tenth as strong here as it is in our time."

"And where—and when—exactly are we?" says Inspector Bubblewrap.

"We're in the future," says Terry. "Almost *sixty-five thousand years* in the future!"

"This is the *worst* time machine ever!" I say.

"No, it's not," says Terry. "It's a *great* time machine. It's just the chronometer that's not working properly."

"Well, it's the worst chronometer ever, then," I say, smashing my head against the control panel in frustration . . .

but my head just bounces off as if the panel was made of marshmallow.

"Stupid reduced gravity!" I shout.

"Look on the bright side, Andy," says Terry. "Reduced gravity is *cool*! Let's get out and have a bounce around."

Terry is in such a hurry to get out that he slips and falls and lands on his head.

"Are you okay?" I say.

"Of course!" says Terry. "It didn't even hurt! Reduced gravity, remember?"

BOING!

I see a flying fried-egg car heading straight toward the inspector. "Watch out!" I say.

My warning comes too late. The car hits the inspector right in the head . . . but it just bounces off!

cloud
(badly
drawn)

"I just got hit by a flying fried-egg car and I didn't feel a thing!" he says. "It would appear that the future is 100 percent danger-proof!"

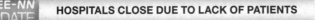

"All right!" says Terry. "Let's party!"

"Look at me! I can run headfirst into this wall and I just bounce off!"

BOING!

"Look at me!" I say. "I'm swimming in a tank full of man-eating sharks but their teeth are made of rubber so they can't eat me!"

"Look at me!" says Inspector Bubblewrap. "I'm totally on fire but there's no heat in the flames so it doesn't hurt a bit!"

"THE 100 PERCENT TOTALLY DANGER-PROOF FUTURE IS AMAZING!" we shout.

Terry runs into the wall again.

I jump back into the shark's mouth.

The inspector sets himself on fire once more.

  BOING! CHOMP! CRACKLE!

And then we do it again . . .

and again . . .

and
again . . .

and
again . . .

and
again . . .

and
again . . .

and
again.

YAWN. YAWN. YAWN. ZZZ. ZZZ. ZZZ.

"I'm bored of running headfirst into a wall without getting hurt," says Terry.

"I'm bored of being chewed by a man-eating shark without getting mangled," I say.

"I'm bored of setting myself on fire without getting burned," says the inspector.

"THE 100 PERCENT DANGER-PROOF FUTURE IS 100 PERCENT BORING!" we shout.

"Why don't we watch TV?" says Terry. "Look, there's one on that tree over there."

"Great idea!" I say. "TV in the future must be amazing!"

"Yes, let's have a look," says the inspector. "Too much TV can ruin the eyes and rot the brain, but a little bit can't hurt . . . particularly now that we are so bored."

"Hooray!" says Terry, scrolling through the menu. "It's time for the *Barky the Barking Dog Show*!"

"Actually," I say, "I think you'll find it's the *Barky the Non-barking Robo-dog Show*."

"In the future, even Barky is boring!" says Terry.

"He's *always* been boring," I say, "but now that they've de-barked him, he's even *more* boring!"

TREE-NN UPDATE **DE-BARKED BARKY BORES EVEN HIS BIGGEST FAN**

"Psst!" whispers a person from the future who looks just like me. "Did you just say 'boring'?"

"Yes," I say. "Are you our future selves?"

"Affirmative," he says. "My name is Android G and this is my friend Terrybot D."

"Cool," says Terry. "Are you guys robots?"

"Well, we do have bionic bits and pieces," explains Terrybot D, "but we're still human enough that we want to have fun."

"But we *can't* have any fun," says Android G. "Because Safety Central Headquarters controls *everything*!"

"Oh my goodness," says Inspector Bubblewrap. "I work for Safety Central Headquarters, but I never dreamed they would become so powerful that they stop people from having any fun at all."

"I know a way we can all have some fun," says Terry. "Let's go to Safety Central Headquarters and destroy it."

"Not so fast, Past Terry," says Terrybot D. "We have to figure out a way to get in there first. It's rhyming-password protected."

"I think I can help you there," says Inspector Bubblewrap. "I wrote that rhyming password. It may have been 65 thousand years ago, but I remember it as if it were only yesterday."

We hop in Android G's flying fried-egg car and fly to Safety Central Headquarters.

Inspector Bubblewrap puts his face up to the panel and says:

Ak to molly to golly go sump,
De ump de yada yahoo.
Sing song yellow belly,
Irrawarra ding dong,
Blibber blabber, jibber jabber, boo!

We all hold our breath . . . and wait.

With a quiet whoosh, the door opens.

"Yay," whispers Terry.

Quickly we follow the inspector down a long shiny corridor and into a vast control room.

There are millions of automated buttons, levers, dials, and switches controlling every aspect of safety in the future.

"Where do we start?" I say. "It looks so complicated!"

"It's not *that* complicated," says the inspector. "There's a master control panel right here."

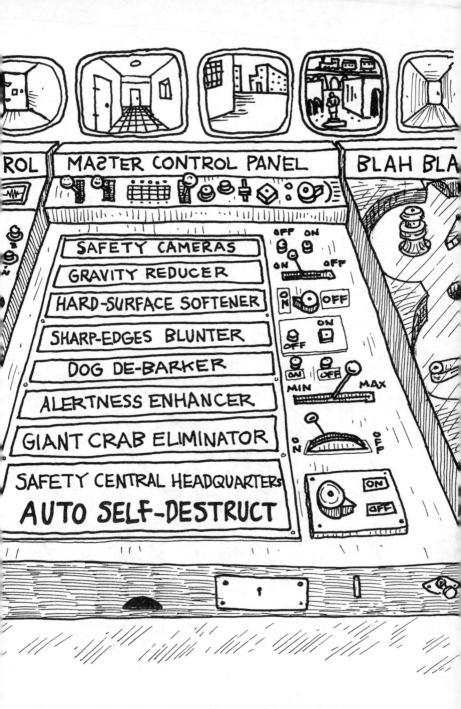

"I can restore earth to its default settings," says the inspector, "by flicking each of the switches from ON to OFF, like so."

"What about the giant-crab eliminator switch?" says Terry.

"No," says the inspector, "I'm going to leave that one on so the earth never gets overrun with giant crabs. But I *am* going to push the self-destruct button so nobody can make the world 100 percent danger-proof ever again. There. All done."

TREE-NN UPDATE **SAFETY CENTRAL HEADQUARTERS SET TO BLOW**

"You mean this whole place is going to blow up?"
I say.

"Yes," says the inspector.

"Cool!" I say. "When?"

"In about ten seconds," says the inspector. "Run!"
We run . . .

and make it out just in time . . .

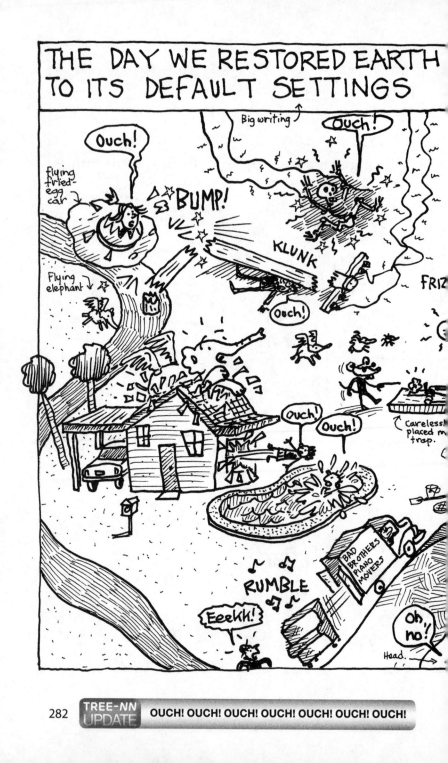

OUCH! OUCH! OUCH! OUCH! OUCH! OUCH! OUCH!

"I think our work here is done," says Terry, as we climb into our bin.

"Yes," says the inspector. "I see now that too much safety is not necessarily a good thing."

"I sure hope we make it to the building permit office this time," I say, as the swirling starts again.

"Me too," says the inspector. "Well . . . sort of . . . I mean . . . time travel is kind of coooooooooooooooooooooooooooooooooooooooooooooooooooooooooooooooooooooooooooooooooooooooooooooooooooooooooooooooooooooooooooooooooooooooooooooooooooooooooooooooooool . . ."

SWIRL!!

CHAPTER 11

THE FUTURE'S FUTURE

We swirl and swirl and swirl some more until we finally stop swirling.

"I've got some good news and some bad news," says Terry, looking out of the bin. "The bad news is we're 650 million years in the future. The good news is we're at the beach."

I look around. It's a weird beach. The sea is black. The sky is red. Oh yeah, and we're surrounded by giant crabs.

"I can't understand why there are giant crabs everywhere," says the inspector. "I'm sure I left the giant-crab eliminator button on back at Safety Central Headquarters."

"Um," says Terry, "I think I *might* have turned it off when you weren't looking. I couldn't help it. I just really wanted to see a giant crab."

TREE-NN UPDATE   **IDIOT SWITCHES GIANT CRAB BUTTON OFF**

"You idiot, Terry!" I say. "Thanks to you the future earth is now overrun with giant crabs."

"Yeah, I know," says Terry, "and I'm sorry. But look on the bright side: giant crabs are pretty cool."

"Yeah, you're right," I say, "they are *extremely* cool . . . and very, very dangerous!"

"It's interesting, though," says Terry, "because this is just like what happens at the end of *The Time Machine* by H. G. Wells. The time traveler goes into the future as far as he can—almost to the end of time—and lands on a beach and there are giant crabs all over the place!"

"I thought that book was fiction," I say.

"So did I!" says Terry. "But it was obviously based on *actual fact*. H. G. Wells must have time-traveled here himself . . . otherwise, how could he have described it all so exactly?"

"Oh dear," says the inspector. "Look over there. One of the giant crabs has got hold of an old-fashioned man and is waving him around in its giant crab claw!"

"That's no *ordinary* old-fashioned man," says Terry. "That's *H. G. Wells.* I recognize him from his author photo on the back cover of the book."

H.G.Wells's future dream balloon

A page of The Time Machine

H.G.Wells's head

H.G.Wells's neck

H.G. Wells's pen

H.G.Wells's table

H.G.Wells's cat

H.G.Wells's chair

H.G.Wells's teacup

TREE-NN UPDATE

H. G. WELLS'S CAT: EXCLUSIVE PIC!

"That's him, all right," I say. "I'd know that mustache anywhere. We'd better go and help him otherwise he won't be able to get back to 1895 to write *The Time Machine* and inspire you to build a time-traveling wheelie bin so that we can go back in time and get our building permit and save the treehouse from being demolished!"

"Leave it to me," says the inspector, leaping out of the bin. "I'll save him!"

"Wait for us!" I say. "You can't fight a crab that big all by yourself!"

But the inspector is already too far ahead—and too excited—to hear me.

"He's really getting into this risk-taking thing, isn't he?" says Terry.

"Yeah," I say. "Maybe a little *too* much. We'd better go and make sure he's okay."

We jump out of the bin and run after him.

"Help me, Man-from-the-future!" calls H. G. Wells as the inspector runs toward him. "I'm caught in a giant crab's claw!"

"Don't worry, Mr. Wells," says the inspector. "I'll save you!"

"How do you know my name?" says H. G. Wells.

"I'll explain later," says the inspector. "First we need to teach this crab some good old-fashioned manners."

Holding his pen and clipboard like a sword and shield, Inspector Bubblewrap rushes toward the crab.

But the crab snatches the inspector up in its other claw and waves him around in the air beside H. G. Wells.

"Oh dear," says Terry. "That didn't work very well at all. Maybe I should try my balloon."

He gets it out of his pocket.

"Hang on," I say. "Snake charming is one thing, but I've never heard of *crab* charming . . . especially not *giant*-crab charming."

"I'm not going to *charm* it," says Terry. "Crabs *hate* the sound of screeching balloons. *Everybody* knows that!"

"I didn't even know crabs *had* ears," I say.

"Well, technically, they don't," explains Terry, "but they can *feel* sound and they don't like the feel of screeching balloons."

TREE-NN UPDATE **SCREECHING BALLOON TO MAKE CRABS CRABBY?**

Terry blows the balloon up, pinches the neck, and releases the air in a high-pitched screech—directly at the crab.

The crab's antennas start whipping around wildly. It shudders, shakes, and sways from side to side.

Terry keeps up the screeching until the crab flings H. G. Wells and the inspector to the ground and scuttles away.

    CRAZED CRAB FLEES CRIME SCENE

"Phew, that was a close shave," says H. G. Wells, standing up and brushing sand off his tweed suit.

"Closer for some than others," says Terry. "Look at the inspector! He's been cut clean in half by the giant crab's claw!"

"Oh no!" I say. "What are we going to do?"

"Bubble wrap," says Terry.

"Good idea," I say. "Popping bubble wrap always calms me down."

"Not for you, Andy," says Terry. "For the inspector. We can use it to join him back up again. Quick! Get his legs and hold them in place."

TREE-NN UPDATE   **BUBBLEWRAP TO BE BUBBLE-WRAPPED**

Terry pulls on the inspector's
roll of bubble wrap
and wraps . . .

and wraps . . .

and wraps.

Finally the inspector is as good as new.

He leaps to his feet and yells: "THAT! WAS! AWESOME! DID YOU SEE ME? I FOUGHT A GIANT CRAB AND I WASN'T EVEN SCARED! LOOK AT THIS SELFIE I TOOK IF YOU DON'T BELIEVE ME!"

BUBBLEWRAP BUBBLE-WRAPPED!

"It was indeed *very* brave," says H. G. Wells, "if not, perhaps, just a *mite* foolhardy. I am, however, forever in your debt, Man-from-the-future, and you two with the magical transparent wrap. Do you live here with the crustaceans?"

"Oh no, we're from the past, too," says Terry, "only not quite as far back as you."

"You're time travelers?" he says.

"Yes," says Terry. "That's our time machine over there. It used to be a wheelie bin. I was inspired to convert it into a time machine after reading your book."

"Which book are you talking about?" says H. G. Wells.

"*The Time Machine*, of course," says Terry.

ILLUSTRATOR INSPIRED BY AUTHOR

"*The Time Machine*?" repeats H. G. Wells slowly. "But I have not written any such book."

"Not yet," I say, "but you will."

"Yes, I believe I will," he says. "That sounds like an excellent idea. I'll write about my time-traveling adventures."

"That's what *we* do," says Terry. "We mostly write about stuff that actually happens to us."

"Yeah," I say. "Why make stuff up when real life is *so* interesting?"

"You're writers, too?" says H. G. Wells.

"Yes," says Terry. "I'm Terry and this is Andy. He does the words and I do the pictures."

"And I inspect buildings," says the inspector. "Inspector Bubblewrap at your service. It's an honor to meet you."

"Well, I'm honored to meet you all as well," says H. G. Wells. "How can I ever repay you for saving me from that monstrous crab-like creature?"

"Could you help us repair our time machine?" says Terry.

"Possibly," says H. G. Wells. "What exactly seems to be the problem?"

"Our chronometer is stuck on the numbers six and five," says Terry. "Only the zeros are moving."

H. G. Wells smiles and nods. "Ah yes, that's happened to me *many* times. Chronometers can be very temperamental . . . Let me have a look at it."

"Here's the problem," says H. G. Wells. "This bit of popcorn was stuck in the perambulic-merimbulator. I've reset the chronometer but it's a little damaged. I'm afraid it will only get you back to the time from which you started your journey."

"Thanks, H. G.," says Terry.

"Yeah, thanks," I say. "We can't get our building permit, but at least we can get back to our time."

"I understand," says H. G. Wells. "I am as eager to return to my time as you are to yours. As you know, I have a novel to write and, as usual, the deadline is looming. And with your permission I'd like to include you in my story and describe your heroic acts."

"That might be a problem," I say. "Our contract with our publisher, Mr. Big Nose, doesn't allow us to appear in anyone else's books."

"I see publishers are no more reasonable in your time than they are in mine," says H. G., nodding. "I guess some things *never* change. Rest assured, I won't mention you in my narrative."

"Does your publisher also have a big nose?" says Terry.

"As a matter of fact, it *is* rather large," says H. G. "I have a picture of him here. See?"

"Yikes!" says Terry.

TREE-NN UPDATE   **PUBLISHER PIC TERRIFIES TERRY**

"Well, all's well that ends well," says H. G. "It's been a pleasure, gentlemen. Good-bye and good time-traveling."

We wave good-bye as H. G. Wells's time machine disappears into the past.

"I wish we could take one of the giant crabs back with us," says Terry.

"Nice idea," I say. "But they are quite dangerous and, besides, there's no way we could fit one in the bin."

"That's a pity," says Terry. "I'd love to see who would win out of a fight between a giant crab and The Trunkinator."

"Yeah, me too!" says the inspector. "That would really be something to see."

We climb into our time machine.

"Hold on tight," says Terry. "Here we go, back to the presentttttttttttttttttttttttttttttttttttttttttttttttttttttt ttttttttttttttttttttttttttttttttttttttttttttttttttttttttttttttttttttttttt ttttttttttttttttttttttttttttttttttttttttttttttttttttttttttttttttttttttttt ttttttttttttttttttttttttttttttttttttttttttttttttttttttttttttttttttttttttt ttttttttttttttttttttttttttttttttttt . . ."

SWIRL!!

CHAPTER 12

BACK TO THE PRESENT

As we swirl our way backward through time, I have my fingers crossed we'll arrive safely back at the treehouse. It feels like we've been away for ages.

"Hey, I can smell marshmallows!" says Terry.
"And lemonade!" says the inspector.

"And chocolate, pizza, ice cream, lollipops, bumper cars, popcorn, and ants!" I say. "We must be getting close to the treehouse!"

I open the lid of the bin and see that, sure enough, we are hurtling straight toward our tree.

Our treehouse.

Our ant farm.

Our ant farm?

OUR ANT FARM!!!

The ant farm that Jill made us promise never to disturb again!!!

"Terry, can you steer us away from the ant farm?" I say. "Into the chocolate fountain instead, maybe? Or the swimming pool?"

"I can't control it," says Terry. "I forgot to ask H. G. Wells to fix the steering. Brace yourselves!"

TREE-NN UPDATE   **TIME TRAVELERS BRACE FOR BUMPY LANDING**

SMASH!

We all fall out of the bin onto the level where the ant farm *used* to be.

There are ants everywhere. Angry ants. Angry ants even angrier than they were before. It doesn't take them long to regroup . . . into a massive angry ant-fist!

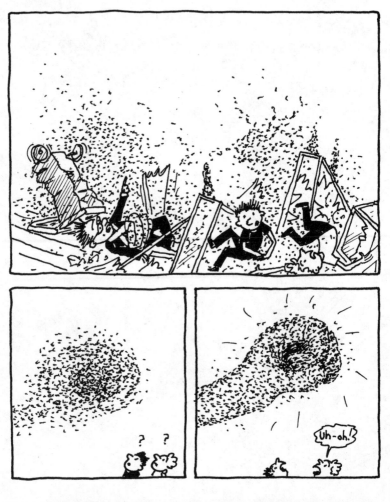

TREE-NN UPDATE   ANT ANGER ESCALATES

The ant-fist rises above us. We shut our eyes and prepare to be ant-fist-punched into oblivion . . .

I wait.

But nothing happens.

I open my eyes.

The ant-fist is still poised above us but it's not coming down.

The inspector seems slightly disappointed.

I look across at Terry. There's a large, weird-looking ant sitting on his head. It's wiggling its antennas toward the ants in the ant-fist.

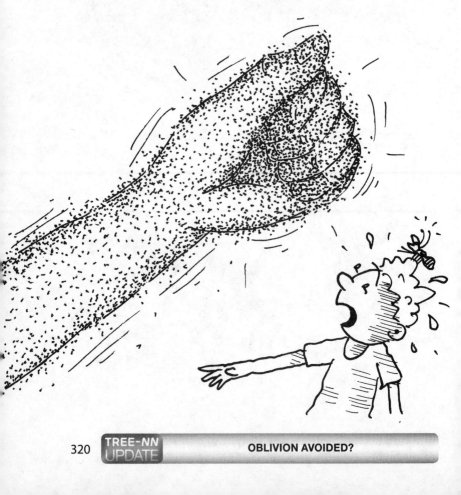

TREE-NN
UPDATE

OBLIVION AVOIDED?

"Is there something on my head?" says Terry.

"Yes," I say. "A big ant. I think it's talking to our ants."

"It must be the prehistoric ant I saved from the exploding Bignoseasaur!" says Terry. "It's been in my pocket the whole time! I forgot all about it!"

"That's not the only thing you forgot about!" says a tiny voice below us.

We look down and see a tiny person with a micro-mini-megaphone.

"Jill?" I say. "Is that you?"

"Of course it's me!" she says. "Where have you been? You went off and left me here all small. I was nearly eaten by a spider, you know. Do you have any idea how scary spiders are when you're the size of an ant?"

"I'm so sorry, Jill!" I say. "We had to go traveling back in time to get a building permit for the treehouse to stop from being demolished, but Terry couldn't control the time machine and we went all over history and into the future and we . . . well . . . sort of forgot all about you."

"Well, that's pretty obvious!" she says.

"We've been on quite a journey, that's true," says the inspector. "But, according to my watch, only a few minutes have passed since we left."

"It's been much longer than that for me," says Jill. "Time passes faster when you're small. I've been living with the ants for a whole year. I thought you were *never* coming back!"

BATTLING A DEADLY ANT-EATING SPIDER.

REMOVING A WANDERING GIANT ANTEATER.

"Will you ever be able to forgive us?" I say.

"Oh, I suppose so," says Jill. "I have to admit it wasn't *all* bad. The real question is whether the ants can forgive you for breaking your solemn promise never to disturb their ant farm ever again."

"It appears they already have," I say. "Well, Terry, at least. Look, they've formed themselves into a massive certific-*ant* of gratitude!"

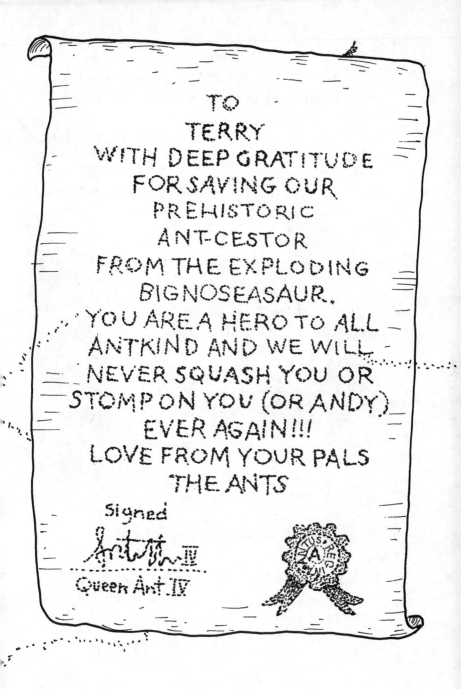

"That is so typical of the ant kingdom," says Jill. "Ants are some of the nicest people I've ever met."

"Would you like me to draw you back to normal size?" says Terry.

"Not right now," says Jill. "There are a few things I need to do and I think the ants are going to need a little help rebuilding their farm. I'll call you on the micro-mini-megaphone when I'm ready."

"Well, that all worked out quite nicely," says Terry.

"Yes," I say, "except we *still* don't have our building permit."

"Oh yeah," says Terry, "I completely forgot. That's why we went time traveling in the first place . . . and now we can't go back because our time machine is broken."

I turn to the inspector. "So do we still need the permit?"

"I'm afraid so," he says. "Without the permit, I can't cancel the demolition. And I can't issue a permit because your treehouse violates almost every section of the building code."*

*Note: See pages 86–93.

  DEMOLITION DANGER: EXTREME!

"But can't you make an exception?" says Terry. "Just this once? You really seemed to enjoy our trip through time and all the dangerous stuff that happened!"

"Well, yes," says the inspector, "but . . ."

"And doing the chariot race was *way* more dangerous than our rocking horse racetrack or bumper car rink," says Terry.

"And that pit of asps makes our snakes and ladders level look as harmless as a petting zoo!" I remind him.

"And aren't you the guy who fought a giant crab?!" says Terry. "Remember this?"

Terry shows the inspector his selfie.

"Yeah," says the inspector. "I did, didn't I? I really did fight a *giant crab*."

"You sure did," I say. "Nobody's ever fought a bigger or more dangerous crab in the history of the entire world."

The inspector rubs his chin thoughtfully. "Well, let's see, I mean given everything that we've been through, I'm prepared to be a *little* bit flexible. I can overlook some things, like the sharks, the bowling alley, and the chain saws . . . but there's absolutely no way I can ignore the fact that you do not have a wheelchair-access ramp, and therefore I simply cannot issue the permit no matter how much I would like to. My hands are tied."

"What if we build one?" I say.

"Well, of course!" says the inspector. "If you build the ramp I can issue the permit and then call off the wrecking crew. But I'm afraid you don't have much time. They'll be here any minute."

"No problem," I say. "We can do it, but we're going to need some extra Andys and Terrys. Come on, Terry! To the cloning machine! We haven't a moment to lose!"

RAMP-BUILDING REPLICAS BUILD RAMP

With the help of our clones—and some of Jill's animals—we build the ramp at super-speed and have it ready just in time for the grand opening.

GRAND WHEELCHAIR-ACCESS RAMP OPENING

CROCODILE PIT →

GRAND OPENING

TREE-NN UPDATE   WORLD'S MOST DANGEROUS RAMP OPENS

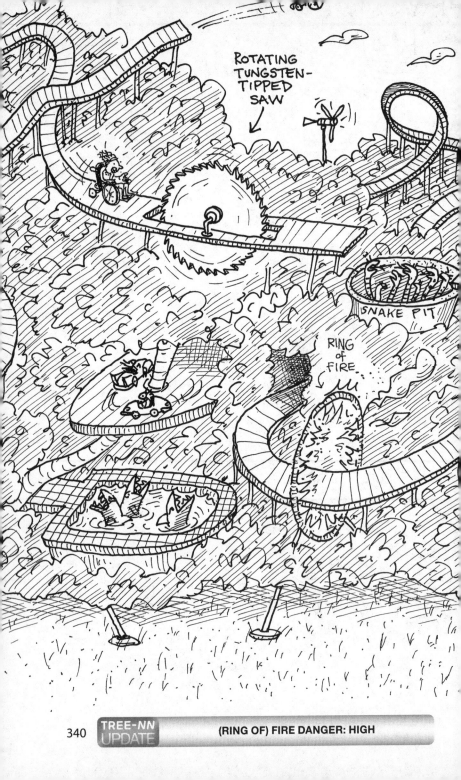

ROTATING
TUNGSTEN-
TIPPED
SAW

SNAKE PIT

RING
of
FIRE

TREE-NN
UPDATE

(RING OF) FIRE DANGER: HIGH

"So," I say to the inspector, "what do you think?"

"I've inspected a lot of ramps in my time," he says, "but this is by far the most dangerous one I've *ever* seen . . . I LOVE it!"

He signs a piece of paper on his clipboard, hands it to us, and says:

"The ramp you've built is perfect
And has earned my stamp of approval,
So your treehouse now has a permit
And there's no need for its removal."

POP
POP

TREE-NN UPDATE **PERMIT SIGNED: TREEHOUSE SAVED!**

"Cool!" says Terry. "We can put the permit on the tree trunk right next to my certific-*ant*."

The inspector shakes our hands and says:

"And now there's nothing for me to do
But to go and cancel the wrecking crew.
And so I take my leave of you,
I bid the two of you adieu."

The inspector grabs a vine and swings down through the leaves and into the forest.

"*Now* can I say it?" says Terry.

"Say what?"

"That everything has worked out quite nicely."

"Not really," I say. "Because there's still one thing we haven't done."

"What thing?" says Terry.

"We still haven't written our book and it's due at twelve o'clock!"

"What time is it now?"

"Almost twelve o'clock."

"Gulp!" says Terry.

CHAPTER 13

THE LAST CHAPTER

"But it will be impossible to do the book by twelve o'clock," says Terry. "We haven't even started it."

"Speak for yourself!" I say. "I've done chapter one and I started chapter two but I had to stop because you were strangling me."

Hey, worms! Stop eating holes in my bowling ball.

"Well, yes, but, *technically*, that wasn't me," says Terry. "It was the ants pretending to be me."

"Well, yes, *technically*, but it was *your* fault the ants were so angry," I remind him.

"Well, *technically*, yes," he says, "but, *technically*, you were responsible for them being angry as well."

"Well, if you want to get *technical* about it, yes, that's true, but it was you who left the gate open."

"Well, *technically*, yes, but, *technically* . . ."

The penguin's distracted. Let's get out of here.

"Excuse me!" shouts Jill through her micro-mini-megaphone. "Can I interrupt for a minute?"

"Well, *technically*, you already have," I say.

"Why don't you just ask the ants to help you?" she says.

"How could *they* help?" I say.

"They're very good at forming words—and pictures—and they can do it very fast," says Jill. "You saw how quickly they made the certific-*ant*."

"But how could they write and illustrate a whole book?" I say. "They don't even know the story."

"Easy," says Jill. "You tell it to me and I'll tell it to them and they'll have it done in no time."

TREE-NN UPDATE TALENTED ANTS TO TELL TREEHOUSE TALE

"Okay," I say. "Well, my name is Andy."

"And I'm Terry," says Terry.

"And we live in a tree . . ." I say.

"Um," says Jill, "I already know all this. You might want to speed it up a bit. Remember, you haven't got much time."

"Good point," I say. "We'll speed-talk it."

"Okay, they're ready," says Jill. "Watch this!"

"Wow! Look at them go!" says Terry. "They're forming the pages right in front of our very eyes!"

CHAPTERS 2 AND 3: EXCLUSIVE PREVIEW!

353

"Okay," says Terry.
"That's fine by me.
Please feel free
To see our tree."

"Well, thank you very much,
Young man.
I'll do my inspection
As fast as I can.

"If I may
I'll start right here.
Uh-oh—oh my—
Oh no—oh dear.

"*This staircase of yours
Should have a railing.
And no wheelchair ramp?
That's a serious failing!*

"*And where are your fire escapes,
Your hose reels and sprinklers,
Your safety blankets and fire extinguishers?
And I'd very much like to see (if I can)
Your in-case-of-emergency exit plan.*

Pretty soon we've built the most amazing 65-story prehistoric pond-scum-puddle sun shelter you've ever seen.

"There you go," says Terry. "That should keep you all sun safe for the next 300 million years or so!"

Clever ants.

Then the one who looks like me starts tugging at *my* pants.

"What's wrong with you stupid things?" I say. "Can't you see we've got a serious problem here?"

"I think they're trying to help us," says the inspector, who has one tugging at his pants as well. "They're pulling us in the direction of that burrow!"

146   HELP AT HAND FOR HAPLESS HEROES

"He's right!" says Terry. "And we don't have a moment to lose. I've never seen a nose so ready to blow!"

AH...AH...AH...   147

I open the lid of the bin. "Wow, look!" I say. "Cavemen!"

"And *cave women*!" says Terry. "And *cave children* and . . . *cave dogs*!"

"They don't look very happy," I say.

"No," says Terry. "They look kind of bored."

160   CAVE PEOPLE ROCK!

BOREDOM DANGER: HIGH   161

It looks like real writing.

Panels (pages 264–265):

and
again . . . **BOING!** **CHOMP!** **CRACKLE!**

and
again . . . **BOING!** **CHOMP!** **CRACKLE!**

and
again . . . **BOING!** **CHOMP!** **CRACKLE!**

and
again . . . **BOING!** **CHOMP!** *YAWN!* **CRACKLE!**

264 TREE-NN UPDATE BOING!CHOMP!CRACKLE!BOING!CHOMP!CRACKLE!

TREE-NN UPDATE BOING!CHOMP!CRACKLE!BOING!CHOMP!CRACKLE! 265

"Oh dear," says Terry. "That didn't work very well at all. Maybe I should try my balloon."

He gets it out of his pocket.

"Hang on," I say. "Snake charming is one thing, but I've never heard of *crab* charming . . . especially not *giant*-crab charming."

"I'm not going to *charm* it," says Terry. "Crabs *hate* the sound of screeching balloons. *Everybody* knows that!"

"I didn't even know crabs *had* ears," I say.

"Well, technically, they don't," explains Terry, "but they can *feel* sound and they don't like the feel of screeching balloons."

296 TREE-NN UPDATE SCREECHING BALLOON TO MAKE CRABS CRABBY!

Terry blows the balloon up, pinches the neck, and releases the air in a high-pitched screech—directly at the crab.

TREE-NN UPDATE SCREEEEEEEEEEEEEEEEEEEEEEEEEEEEEEEEEEECH! 297

Are you made of ant writing?

Me! Made of ants? I DON'T KNOW!!!!

"That's our best book *ever*," I say. "And to think that it's all made by ants! But how are we going to get it to Mr. Big Nose on time?"

"I know!" says Terry. "Let's go ask the three wise owls."

"Do you really think that's such a good idea?" says Jill.

"Yes," says Terry. "They're *very* wise."

"I'm not so sure about that," says Jill.

"But they were the ones who suggested we go time traveling to get our permit," I say, "and that was a good idea . . . well, sort of."

"All right," says Jill. "I guess it can't hurt." She jumps onto my shoulder and we all head up to the wise owls' house.

"O wise owls," says Terry, "how can we get our book to Mr. Big Nose on time?"

TREE-NN UPDATE   WISE OWLS CONSULTED ON DELIVERY DILEMMA

"What are they trying to tell us?" I say.

"I don't know," says Terry, "but it sounds *very* wise."

"Not to me, it doesn't," says Jill. "It just sounds like they're saying random words."

"They're not random," says Terry. "You put them together and they reveal a hidden meaning."

"Okay," says Jill. "What's the hidden meaning of 'Cheese sticks, elbow, hoo, blibber, blabber, bloo, chicken, chutney, poop-poop'?"

Terry looks at me.

I look at Terry.

We both shrug.

Suddenly we hear a loud roar, and a motorbike flies through the leaves of the tree and skids to a stop in front of us.

The rider dismounts and removes his helmet.

"Inspector Bubblewrap?!" I say.

TREE-NN
UPDATE
BIKING BUBBLEWRAP BURSTS IN!

"At your service," he says. "But I'm not an inspector anymore—I'm a stuntman. You can call me Super BW from now on. The BW stands for *bubble wrap*."

"But safety is your life," says Terry.

"It *was* my life," says Super BW, "but I've swapped my hard hat for a helmet and decided to become a stuntman. I came back to thank you both for changing my life for the better. But what's the matter? You look worried."

"It's our new book," I say. "We have to get it to Mr. Big Nose in less than one minute but his office is in the city on the other side of the forest!"

FRUCTOSE!

FRUIT TINGLES!

POOP-POOP!

"Sounds like a job for Super BW," he says. "I'll not only get it there on time, but I'll do it in the most spectacularly dangerous and thrilling way possible. Your new wheelchair-access ramp will be perfect for a stunt like this."

Super BW takes our book, puts on his helmet, remounts his bike, and rides out of the tree and into the forest to get the longest run-up possible.

"Clear the ramp!" I say. "Super BW is coming through!"

We hear the revving of his bike's engine and then Super BW comes speeding up the ramp . . . shoots off up into the air . . .

TREE-NN UPDATE FIVE . . . FOUR . . . THREE . . . TWO . . . ONE . . .

flies over the forest, toward the city . . .

and approaches the office of Big Nose Books where Mr. Big Nose is sitting at his desk, watching Super BW come closer . . .

and closer . . .   and closer . . .

TREE-NN UPDATE   VRROOOOOOOOOOOOOOOOOOOOOOOOOOOOOOOM!

until he smashes through the window . . .

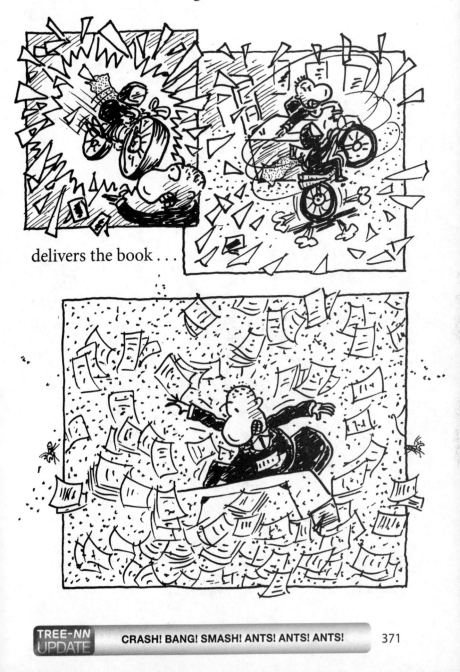

delivers the book . . .

and then rides out again!

"THAT! WAS! AMAZING!" says Terry.

"Yeah," I say, "I've never seen a jump like it. But when he threw the book on Mr. Big Nose's desk, the ants went everywhere."

"Don't worry," says Jill. "They'll remember their places and get back into position very quickly. Can you draw me normal size again please, Terry?"

"Sure," he says.

"May I keep the micro-mini-megaphone, though?" says Jill. "It will come in handy for talking to giraffes."

"And giants," I say.

I fixed Jill.

megaphone

What about her other leg?

"Speaking of gi-*ants*," says Jill, "I'd better be getting back to my pet salon. I've promised the prehistoric ant that I'll update his hairstyle—the one he has at the moment is a little old-fashioned!"

TREE-NN UPDATE · **NEW LOOK FOR OLD ANT**

"Well," I say, after Jill has gone, "I guess we'd better be getting up to Tree-NN. We've got some important news to announce."

"What?" says Terry.

"That we're going to add another 13 stories to the treehouse!"

"Yay!" says Terry. "A 78-story treehouse. Can one of the new stories be a drive-through car wash that we can drive through with the windows down? I've *always* wanted to try that!"

"Me too!" I say. "Let's do it!"

THE END

Andy Griffiths lives in a 65-story treehouse with his friend Terry and together they make funny books, just like the one you're holding in your hands right now. Andy writes the words and Terry draws the pictures. If you'd like to know more, read this book (or visit www.andygriffiths.com.au).

Terry Denton lives in a 65-story treehouse with his friend Andy and together they make funny books, just like the one you're holding in your hands right now. Terry draws the pictures and Andy writes the words. If you'd like to know more, read this book (or visit www.terrydenton.com).

Thank you for reading
this FEIWEL AND FRIENDS book.
The Friends who made

THE 65-STORY TREEHOUSE

possible are:

Jean Feiwel, Publisher
Liz Szabla, Editor in Chief
Rich Deas, Senior Creative Director
Holly West, Editor
Alexei Esikoff, Senior Managing Editor
Kim Waymer, Production Manager
Anna Roberto, Editor
Christine Barcellona, Associate Editor
Emily Settle, Administrative Assistant
Anna Poon, Editorial Assistant

Follow us on Facebook or visit us online at mackids.com.
Our books are friends for life